PIG the PUG

D0413444

For my parents.
And all those little dogs.
A.B.

First published in 2014 by Scholastic Press
An imprint of Scholastic Australia Pty Limited

First published in the UK in 2015 by
Scholastic Children's Books
Euston House
24 Eversholt Street
London NW1 1DB
A division of Scholastic Ltd
www.scholastic.co.uk

London • New York • Toronto • Sydney • Auckland
Mexico City • New Delhi • Hong Kong

Text and illustrations ©Aaron Blabey 2014

All rights reserved

ISBN 978 1407 15498 5

Printed in China

9 10 8

The moral rights of Aaron Blabey have been asserted.

Papers used by Scholastic Children's Books are made from wood grown in sustainable forests.

PIG the PUG

Aaron Blabey

SCHOLASTIC

Pig was a Pug
and I'm sorry to say,
he was greedy and selfish
in most every way.

He lived in a flat
with a sausage dog, Trevor.
But when was he nice to him?
I'll tell you–NEVER.

'You've got some great toys there,'
poor Trevor would say.

But Pig would just grumble,
'They're mine! **GO AWAY!**'

'But it might be more fun,' said Trevor to Pig,
'if we both played together...'

Well, Pig flipped his wig.

'No, they are mine!
Are you deaf? Only mine!
You keep your paws off them,
you sausage-shaped swine!

I know what your game is,
you want me to **SHARE!**
But I'll never do that!
I WON'T and **I SWEAR!**'

And with that, he proceeded to gather his stuff

and make a big pile, with a huff and a puff.

And once he had gathered them
up in a pile,
he howled from the top
with a satisfied smile.

'*There!*' shouted Pig.
'Now you won't get my loot!
It's **MINE! MINE! MINE! MINE!**
So why don't you *SCOOT?!*'

But just at that moment
poor Trevor did see,
the pile was wobbling.

Oh dear me.

'Watch out up there!' good Trevor did cry.
But the shame of it was...

Well, pigs cannot fly.

These days it's different,
I'm happy to say.
It's so very different
in most every way.

Yes, Pig shares his toys now,
and Trevor's his friend.
And they both play together…

...while Pig's on the mend.